Dear H

It looks like the threat King Ivar made last time you were here has come true. He's got hold of the ultimate power now, according to the unicorns, and everyone's saying that means he will be impossible to defeat. But you were such a great Guardian when I met you that I know you'll try your hardest to beat him.

The other problem is that lots of creatures are also telling stories about King Ivar trapping their friends. There are plenty of rumours flying around that he's making them become his followers in a new kingdom . . .

I really hope you can come back to Bellua soon. Mith says she'll be waiting for you too!

Billy the Faun

Read all the adventures of

The Phoenix's Flame

CLAIRE TAYLOR-SMITH

Illustrated by Lorena Alvarez

PUFFIN

PUFFIN BOOKS

UK | USA | Canada | Ireland | Australia
India | New Zealand | South Africa

Puffin Books is part of the Penguin Random House group of companies whose
addresses can be found at global.penguinrandomhouse.com.

puffinbooks.com

First published 2015
002

Set in 14.5/24 pt Bembo Book MT Std
Printed in Great Britain by Clays Ltd, St Ives plc

A CIP catalogue record for this book is available from the British Library

ISBN: 978-0-141-35242-8

www.greenpenguin.co.uk

To my bestie, Clare-Bear –

thanks for all your love and support

xxx

Julie and Zoe –

best friends in the whole wide world!

xxx

Winter
Mountains

Cave

Valley
of the
Guardians

Pixie
Park

Elf
Avenue

Dragon's
Valley

Silvery Stream

Unicorn
Meadows

Enchanted
Orchard

Contents

Hanging Out

It was a sunny Friday afternoon, and Hattie Bright and her best friend, Chloe, were sprawled on Hattie's bed, surrounded by a pile of magazines.

'Another week of school over,' sighed Hattie happily. 'I can't wait for two whole days of chilling out!'

'Me neither,' agreed Chloe. 'It was really nice of your mum to invite me for tea today too.'

'Perfect end to the week!' said Hattie.

She slotted her MP3 player into her stereo and chose her favourite song. A happy beat filled the room. The two girls jumped off the bed and began dancing around, as if they were shaking off a week's worth of schoolwork.

As the song finished, Chloe did a crazy spin, and the two friends ended up in a giggly heap on the floor.

'Oh!' said Hattie. 'You're on my wrist!' She laughed as she tried to pull her right arm free from beneath her friend's leg.

'Is that what it is? Sorry!' said Chloe, giggling and rolling to one side.

'Too much dancing,' replied Hattie. As she said that, she could feel a funny warm tingling sensation creeping along her other arm.

3

Chloe got up and went over to the stereo, choosing another song from Hattie's playlist.

Hattie glanced at her left wrist, where she always wore her favourite charm bracelet. The six charms were swinging gently. And, just as Hattie suspected, they had started to glow a warm yellowy-orange.

Her stomach did a flip. She wasn't sure if it was nerves or excitement, but she was certain of one thing: the evil Imp King Ivar had stolen another power from one of the creatures in the magical Kingdom of Bellua. That meant they needed her there . . . now!

As Guardian of Bellua's magical creatures, only Hattie could cure Ivar's latest victim.

Not only that, but when she was last in Bellua the Imp King had threatened the next power he would steal would be the 'ultimate' one – stronger than any of the five he'd taken already!

Hattie shivered. Had Ivar succeeded in his quest? Would it finally be impossible to defeat him? There was only one way to find out. She had to go to Bellua right away! But how could she grab the old vet's bag hidden under her bed and let it secretly transport her to Bellua when Chloe was *right there* in the room?

Hattie knew she couldn't wait until Chloe went home after tea – that would be leaving it dangerously late.

Think, think! she said to herself, squeezing her eyes tightly shut.

There had to be a way to get to Bellua and still keep the secret oath. Hattie only needed Chloe to leave the room for a few minutes – long enough for her to go to Bellua and return as if nothing had happened.

'I love this one, don't you?' said Chloe, as a new song burst from the stereo. She began dancing around the bedroom again. 'Come on, Hattie. On your feet, lazybones!'

But Hattie stayed right where she was on the bedroom floor, looking at her bracelet.

'Er, actually I don't know if I do like this one that much – and anyway it's probably nearly time for tea. Can you go down and ask my mum when it'll be ready while I choose another song?'

'OK then,' agreed Chloe, smiling at Hattie. 'But I'm trusting you to make a good choice!'

Hattie jumped up and busied herself with the stereo, while Chloe slipped out of the room and headed downstairs.

With her heart pounding, Hattie hurried to her bed and reached under it. From downstairs she could hear the muffled voices of Chloe and her mum. She pulled the bag out from its hiding place and dropped it on to the bed.

Quickly, she pressed the glowing star charm on her bracelet against the bag's star-shaped lock. It clicked open immediately and, as the bag began to sparkle and shimmer, Hattie strained her ears for any sound of Chloe making her way back up the stairs. Was that a creak?

Hattie didn't have time to check. She grasped the bag firmly and pulled it wide open. Then she peered inside and found herself tumbling down, down and down . . .

'Your mum says tea's in ten minutes, Hattie!' called Chloe as she pushed the bedroom door open. 'Hattie? Hattie, where are you?'

Chloe glanced towards the silent stereo, then at Hattie's empty bed.

What's that sparkly silver bag doing there? she wondered. She couldn't remember seeing it in the room before. Chloe moved closer to the bag and looked inside, then gasped as she took in the

strangest sight she'd ever seen – Hattie's blue trainers disappearing into the bottom!

'H-Hattie?' she whispered, her voice trembling. 'A-are you i-in there?'

Chloe knew the question was ridiculous so wasn't surprised when there was no answer. With shaking hands, she picked up the bag and gazed at the spot where Hattie's shoes had been. Suddenly she had the strangest sensation. Her whole body tingled and she felt as though something invisible was pulling her into the bag.

Then she felt herself tumbling down, down and down . . .

New Arrival

'A perfect landing!' cried Hattie, as both her feet hit the floor of the Guardian's cave. 'I've finally got –'

She was interrupted by a second thud behind her and spun round to see what had caused it. At first Hattie stood there, her mouth wide open, unable to speak. Then one word came out in a sort of high-pitched squeak: '*Chloe?*'

'Hattie?' said Chloe, looking all around her and taking in the crystal-studded cave walls, the shelves crowded with potion bottles and the huge stone table in front of her. 'Where are we? This is just – just – *wow!*'

Chloe's eyes were wide with wonder, though Hattie could see a flicker of confusion cross her best friend's face too.

Hattie felt her breathing quicken. 'But, Chloe, how did . . . ? What were you . . . ? You can't . . .' Her head was spinning. Chloe couldn't be in Bellua! Hattie had broken the Guardian's oath of secrecy in the worst possible way!

Suddenly, all the words Chloe had been storing up seemed to tumble out in one go, as she pointed towards the sparkly vet's bag on the stone table in front of her.

'I just picked it up, the bag I mean, and I looked inside. Sorry, Hattie, I didn't mean to be nosy, and I know it sounds crazy, but I thought I saw your trainers disappearing . . . I'm almost sure I did . . . And then I felt . . . It was the weirdest thing . . . I couldn't stop it and then . . . and then I ended up here . . .' Chloe caught her breath before asking, 'Where are we anyway?'

Hattie heard a slight tremble in Chloe's voice and put a reassuring arm round her friend's shoulder.

'We're in the magical Kingdom of Bellua,' explained Hattie. 'I, er, I come here sometimes, to sort of . . . help. I look after the creatures here – they're magical ones.'

Chloe tilted her head questioningly.

'I know it sounds silly,' said Hattie, who thought she may as well have told Chloe they were about to have tea with some aliens on Mars, 'but you'll just have to believe me. And you can't tell anyone about it – you really can't. You can't stay here either. It's not allowed. You'll have to try to –' Hattie was distracted by a sliver of light falling across the table as the cave door opened.

'Hattie, you're here already!' called a friendly voice, and Mith Ickle flew over and curled herself round Hattie's shoulders.

Chloe grabbed on to the table edge, as though she might faint from surprise at seeing a small pink dragon greeting her best friend in such a familiar way.

A second later Billy the faun bounded through the door, carrying a beautiful, elegant bird on his shoulder.

The bird's feathers reminded Hattie of a roaring fire – a mix of the brightest orange and yellow. On its head, she noticed that its crest of small feathers was lying flat, as though the bird didn't quite have the energy to hold them upright. Its plump body had sunk heavily on to its golden-scaled legs.

As Chloe gasped in wonder, Hattie knew at once that the downcast bird was her next patient.

'Mith and Billy – Chloe,' said Hattie, introducing her friends to each other. 'Chloe – Mith and Billy.'

'Nice to meet you, Chloe,' said Billy rather formally, then, noticing her look him up and down at least twice, he grinned and added: 'Yes, I'm a faun. Half-boy, half-goat. But you can just think of me as a kid!'

The joke seemed to relax everyone and, for the first time since Chloe's arrival, Hattie saw her smile.

Hattie turned to the bird perched on Billy's shoulder. Its bright yellow eyes were lowered and it looked terribly miserable.

'This is Magenta,' Mith Ickle said.

Billy helped Magenta hop on to the table, her brown talons slipping a little on the stone surface.

'What can I do to help you?' asked Hattie. 'Has King Ivar been causing trouble again?'

Magenta looked up. 'I'm afraid he's stolen an incredibly precious feather from my tail,' she whispered. 'Now he has the ultimate power. I'm a phoenix, you see. I can turn myself into a pile of ash when I get hurt or old. Then I can be reborn from the ashes, stronger than ever. It's a wonderful power – it means that I'm immortal.'

Hattie gasped. 'Oh! So now King Ivar is immortal too?'

Magenta nodded sadly. 'It means he can never come to real harm – or at least if he does he can just start all over again because he's immortal now. You see, only a single creature in Bellua can ever have the power of rebirth at any one time. If you can help me to get my power back, Ivar will lose it immediately – and he won't be invincible any more!'

'Don't worry, Magenta – we can fix this! How did he steal the power from you?' asked Hattie.

'You see this gap in my tail?' said Magenta, twisting round. 'That's where my rebirth feather normally sits. It's the only one with a purple tinge and the one that holds the magic power that allows me to be reborn.'

As Magenta told her story, Hattie took a magnifying glass from the bowl of instruments on the table and examined Magenta's tail. Sure enough, there was a tiny gap in the middle, among the tail feathers.

'I was about to fly home yesterday from Pixie Park,' Magenta continued, 'when Ivar crept up on me and stood on my tail. My rebirth feather was plucked out as I flew away and Ivar grabbed it before I could turn back. Then he ran off, shouting that nobody could ever defeat him now. And the thing is, Hattie, I think he's probably right.'

Hattie felt her stomach do a flip, but then she took a deep breath and reached for the worn red book that had guided her on so many adventures in Bellua before.

'That's the biggest book I've ever seen!' said Chloe, as she helped Hattie to lower it gently on to the stone table.

Hattie smiled. 'It's my book of cures. Now,' she said to Magenta, as confidently as she could, 'let's think about repairing your tail before we worry about Ivar.' She opened the book. 'It has to say *something* in here about restoring a phoenix's power of rebirth. Let's have a look.'

When Hattie finally found the page on curing a phoenix, only one cure was listed: *Restoratione of the supreme power of rebirthing*.

'I suppose you can cure everything else yourself by starting again,' noted Hattie, and Magenta nodded.

'But there's nothing to tell you what to do,' began Chloe, who was peering curiously over Hattie's shoulder at the almost blank page. Then she exclaimed 'Oh!' as pictures and the words of a poem in neat writing gradually began to appear:

For loss of feather, a simple cure,
no lotions or potions can it restore.
The purple plume, it must be found,
and reattached is thus safe and sound.

'So all we have to do is find the lost feather,' said Hattie, before adding with a shiver, 'The only problem is, we'll have to find Ivar for that.'

She was about to close the book when she noticed some more words appearing. In large capitals, the heading was underlined twice:

TREATMENTE OF THOSE WHO STEALE THE ULTIMATE POWER

Hattie clapped with excitement as even more words followed the heading.

'There might be a way to stop Ivar after all! Maybe even for good!'

Chloe looked a little puzzled, but Hattie could see the eyes of Mith Ickle, Billy and Magenta light up with hope.

'It's all explained here . . .' she said, before reading on.

Dark Destinations

The first sentence that Hattie read aloud was a clear warning:

He who takes the power of rebirth through unfair meanes must not be allowed to prosper, for he will wreake certain havoc on the magickal Kingdom of Bellua.

'It's true,' said Mith Ickle, her wings fluttering nervously. 'Ivar's already causing more trouble than ever. He's been snatching creatures wherever he goes and insisting that they're going to be his first loyal citizens when

he takes control of the whole kingdom. A party of pixies told me he trapped a group of their friends in an enchanted flower circle. He took them off somewhere, cackling about his "lovely new followers".'

'It's not just pixies,' added Billy. 'I've heard rumours that he caught a shimmer of sprites in a net and tricked a couple of elves into a deep sleep before whisking them away. He even tripped up a young unicorn so that she fell into a trap and couldn't get out.' Billy shook his head gravely. 'None of them have been seen since.'

'Um . . . pixies? Elves? And unicorns?' murmured Chloe, who was listening to the conversation intently.

'Yes, they all live here in Bellua,' confirmed Hattie, before continuing in a more serious tone: 'It looks like Ivar's getting closer to taking over the kingdom then. Not that I'll *ever* let that happen!'

Billy and Mith Ickle nodded in agreement, and Hattie noticed Chloe looking at her admiringly. She hoped she could be as brave as she sounded, as she took a deep breath and read on:

This threat may end by a potion pure,
That brings the thief the strongest cure.
A unicorne hair, a spring-water splash,
All mixed together with phoenix ash.

'A unicorn hair? Oh, I'm sure Themis will give you one,' said Mith Ickle excitedly.

'And you could ask Archie for some spring water,' added Billy.

'Who are Themis and Archie?' asked Chloe.

'Oh, just a unicorn I know and a pegasus I cured,' replied Hattie, as though she was describing a couple of new school friends.

Chloe opened her mouth, then slowly closed it again.

'But I can't give you any phoenix ash,' whispered Magenta with a sniff. 'Not until I get my feather back anyway.'

'Then let's worry about that first,' said Hattie firmly. 'We'll find Ivar, force him to hand it over and have your powers back to full strength before you know it!'

That was another promise Hattie hoped she could keep – but she wasn't at all sure where to begin! Where in the whole kingdom should she start looking for Ivar?

Hattie spread out the map of Bellua that, as usual, had sprung from the pages of the big red book. She began tracing her finger over it, from Unicorn Meadows to the Rainbow Waterfall, and from the Winter Mountains to the Frozen Merlakes. The problem was, she thought, Ivar could be almost anywhere!

As if reading her mind, Billy jumped in and pointed at the map.

'We should probably try the Secret Forest first,' he said. 'That's where Ivar's den is.'

'Yes, yes,' agreed Mith Ickle. 'Maybe he's there guarding the creatures he's taken?' She angrily puffed out a snort of smoke.

'The Secret Forest?' replied Hattie, her eyes darting across the map. 'I can't see it anywhere.'

Billy laughed. 'That's how it got its name. It's so secret it never appears on *any* maps.'

'It's just beyond the Rainbow Waterfall,' said Mith Ickle. 'You can't see it until you're almost in it. Most creatures don't go anywhere near that area, though.'

'But *we* will,' said Hattie firmly. 'Come on, Mith, Billy – let's get ready to go. Magenta, you'd better stay here to save your strength. Is that OK?' The phoenix nodded weakly.

'What about me? How can I help?' said Chloe in a small voice.

Turning to her best friend, Hattie said, 'I'm really sorry, Chloe. I'm going to have to find a way to send you back to our world. You can't stay here – I'll get into *so* much trouble.'

Hattie offered the vet's bag to Chloe. 'Try peering inside again. It worked in one direction for you, so it should work in the other.'

But Chloe didn't move, and Hattie saw the corners of her mouth turn down.

'Can't I stay, now I'm here?' asked Chloe. '*Please?*'

Hattie thought for a moment. As Chloe had already seen the cave and everything in it, was there such a rush for her to leave?

'I know!' said Hattie. 'Why don't you stay here and look after Magenta? I'll be back as soon as I can, but don't leave the cave!'

Hattie saw Chloe's head drop and she gave her friend's arm a light squeeze. 'Sorry, Chloe, it's just so dangerous out there. If anything happened to you, I'd feel terrible. Stay here with Magenta. I won't be long.'

'*Pleeeeease*, Hattie,' Chloe pleaded. 'Let me come. I won't get in the way, I promise! I might even be able to help you.'

Hattie looked at Mith Ickle and Billy, but both of them shrugged.

'Best friends together forever?' added Chloe, raising her eyebrows.

Hattie twisted her mouth from side to side. 'OK then. But you have to promise to do what I say, whatever happens. And to *never* tell *anyone* where you've been.'

'Promise!' said Chloe.

Hattie nodded and put the vet's bag down.

Then Chloe linked arms with her best friend, ready to follow Mith Ickle and Billy through the cave door. 'What are we waiting for, Hattie? Let's go!'

Greetings and Gifts

As they stepped from the cave into the Valley of the Guardians, Hattie beamed at Chloe's gasps of delight at the beautiful sights. Hattie had almost forgotten how wonderful the Kingdom of Bellua was — especially when you were seeing it for the very first time.

'Wow, this is *amazing*!' exclaimed Chloe.

She pulled away from Hattie and began waving her hands through the lightly shimmering air. She skipped through the Valley of the Guardians, pointing excitedly at bright rainbows emerging from pastel clouds, and sighing happily as magical creatures of all shapes and sizes darted and flew around her.

'Elves, unicorns and fairies really exist then,' she said, shaking her head in disbelief. 'I thought they were only in books!'

'Me too – until I came here,' said Hattie. 'And now some of them have become very good friends of mine.'

Mith Ickle fluttered on to Hattie's shoulder as she spoke, nuzzling her neck.

'We should probably get going,' said Billy. 'It's pretty gloomy in the Secret Forest so we need to get there while it's still bright and sunny.'

'You're right,' agreed Hattie, hooking her arm back through Chloe's. She led her friend towards the ornate arch that marked the entrance to Unicorn Meadows.

'My dear Hattie, welcome back!' Themis stepped forward from a group of unicorns. 'We are so happy to see you again. You know that the Imp King has one of our own held captive? We will offer any support we can to help you defeat him and secure her release.'

'Thank you, Themis, I'll remember that,' Hattie said to the leader of the unicorns. 'See you soon – with good news, I hope.'

'This Ivar sounds really scary,' said Chloe quietly as they waved goodbye. Hattie nodded and put a comforting arm round her friend.

Hattie and her friends had barely made their way out of Unicorn Meadows when a group of dragons swooped out of Dragon's Valley.

'Hattie!' called a large red dragon. 'We've just found out that Ivar caught one of our young dragons with a sudden water spring. He was so surprised that he flapped and fluttered right through it. He was so flustered at being

wet that he couldn't stop Ivar taking him prisoner. Nobody knows where he is.'

Hattie thought she heard Mith Ickle sob slightly. 'We'll find him, don't worry!' she said, as cheerfully as she could.

'Thank you, Hattie,' said a spotty second

dragon, who flew towards her bearing a small pot of fruit.

'Stinkberries?' asked Hattie, screwing up her nose.

The dragon shook her head. 'Not this time. They're startleberries. Throw them at the feet of your enemy and they'll snap and whizz. They'll make anyone jump! Hope they help.'

'Thanks! I'm sure they will. We'd better keep going, so we'll say bye for now.'

Mith Ickle wrapped herself round Hattie's shoulders for comfort as the group marched on towards the Enchanted Orchard.

It took a while to get past the orchard and along the Silvery Stream. Every few steps, another creature stopped Hattie to tell her of others who had disappeared.

'We've lost so many friends,' cried one pixie. 'I hope you can help us!'

'He's taken over twenty fairies already,' said a curly-haired one, delicately dabbing at her eyes. 'Will you be able to get them back?'

'One minute my family was behind me and the next *he* had them trapped in a huge filthy bag,' sobbed a brightly dressed elf.

Hattie reassured every creature as best she could. And, as she waved goodbye to them, Hattie felt more determined than ever to find Ivar and to put a stop to his evil plans once and for all.

Eventually, Hattie and Chloe found themselves at Troll Bridge. Stopping to wait for Billy and Mith Ickle to catch up, Hattie spotted a group of trolls walking towards her.

'I really haven't got time for any riddles today. The trolls love them, you see,' Hattie whispered to a trembling Chloe. However, as the trolls got closer she saw that, although their features were still heavy and rather gnarled, all of them were smiling for once.

'Hello, Hattie!' called a plump bald-headed troll. 'Give her the thing, Ginger, give her the thing.'

'The what?' said a short red-haired troll who had a small box tucked under one arm.

'In the box!' said the bald troll, pointing.

'The box? Which box?'

'How about the one under your arm?'

'Oh yes, that one!' The red-haired troll pulled the box out and held it towards Hattie, who hoped he hadn't been holding it too close to his armpit.

'We've saved you some special rocks from inside the Rumbling Volcano, where the stinkiest gases form,' said Ginger. 'Warm these rocks up a bit and the pong will send anyone running.'

Hattie said a grateful thanks as Billy and Mith Ickle joined her. She was just about to set off again when she heard a loud '*Pssssst!*'

She looked all around to see where it was coming from and had almost given up when she spotted something black and shiny scuttling towards her from behind a large rock. Though Chloe jumped in fear, Hattie knew who it was.

'Onyx?' she said with some surprise, as the chief of the shimmer spiders stared back at her with his huge eyes. 'I thought you never left your lair!'

'Only in the most serious of situations,' said Onyx. 'We heard that you were going to face King Ivar, which is a brave thing to do, and I wanted you to have this, Hattie. It's a spool of our magic thread – extra strong and extra sticky, just in case you need it.'

Hattie thanked Onyx and hurried onwards
with her friends, in the direction of the Ancient
Desert. She was relieved to see the sphinxes
were already there, waiting to speed them
across the sands to the Rainbow Waterfall.

Chloe couldn't help but gasp and gaze in wonder at the enormous magical creatures. The sphinxes had the bodies of giant graceful lions, as well as a huge pair of soft wings.

Both girls climbed on gratefully and before long they were on their way. Billy and Mith Ickle trotted and flapped alongside, until the sphinxes gently let their passengers down at the base of the waterfall.

'It's beautiful!' exclaimed Chloe, but Hattie's attention was drawn not to the bright mingling colours of the water but to a large gleaming golden shell perched on a nearby rock. Propped against the shell was a piece of card, with a message written on it in sparkling gold ink:

Hattie, we can't leave the frozen lakes long enough to greet you, but please accept this gift. If you need help from someone, call their name into the shell and they will immediately come to your aid. Your friends, the mermaids x

Hattie picked up the shell, which magically shrank at her touch. The mermaids might be grumpy at times, she thought, but they weren't all bad. Then she slid the now-little shell into her pocket and gathered everyone round, ready to face the next part of their journey.

They were approaching the edge of the Secret Forest, where King Ivar lived . . .

Smoke Signals

As they entered the Secret Forest, Hattie and Chloe both shivered. Almost immediately, the ground beneath their feet felt harder and rougher, and the light sparkly air turned grey and foggy. The trees were heavy with large ragged-edged leaves, their colour a dull muddy green.

'It's this way to Ivar's den,' said Billy, parting some of the branches and guiding the group deeper into the dense forest. 'Follow me!'

They walked round tall trees with twisting boughs and shorter ones with huge low-hanging branches. The air was cool and Hattie could feel Chloe still shivering beside her. The two friends linked arms as they followed Billy and were grateful when Mith Ickle flew above, blowing warm air over them.

They walked further into the forest, taking care to avoid sharp bushes and low branches.

Finally, they reached a clearing and Hattie knew they'd found the den at last. It was smaller than Hattie had expected – not much bigger than the shed in her garden at home. Very cautiously, the group made their way towards it.

'Ugh, it feels disgusting!' exclaimed Chloe, who had accidentally brushed one arm against the slimy yellow moss that was growing up the dried-mud walls.

Hattie gave her friend a sympathetic smile.

'No sign of Ivar then?' asked Billy.

'Not yet,' replied Hattie. 'But I don't think he'll stay away for long – and he's not going to be happy when he spots us lurking around.'

She peered through the den's windows, but the glass was so filthy she couldn't see much inside.

'Should we try knocking on the front door?' suggested Mith Ickle.

'Yes, let's do that,' agreed Hattie, but then something at the side of the den caught her eye.

Hattie and her friends crept round the corner and they all exclaimed in shock when they saw what Ivar had done.

Just behind the Imp King's lair, several wooden posts had been pushed into the ground. Tied to them were many creatures of different shapes and sizes, though none looked hurt. As Hattie approached, their anxious faces turned to her at once.

'Oh, Hattie! We're so pleased to see you!' puffed a young dragon with large purple eyes.

'Are you here to rescue us?' asked a tiny fairy, waving a badly bent wand hopefully.

'Ivar says that if we try to escape he'll put a nasty spell on us that can never be broken,' added a green-suited elf, whose pointed hat was sitting wonkily on one side of his head. 'He says we're to be the first loyal citizens of the new Kingdom of the Important Imp Ivar.'

'"*The Kingdom of the Important Imp Ivar*", eh?' said Hattie, shaking her head. 'If you can wait quietly just a little longer, I'll try to set you free as soon as I can.' Then she put a finger to her lips before turning to her friends.

'We've got to act quickly,' she said.

With that, she walked as confidently as she could towards Ivar's front door.

'Ivar, are you in there? Come out – I need to talk to you!'

As she approached, the toadstools that grew on either side of the door hissed menacingly. Hattie jumped back in surprise. She tried walking round the whole den instead, calling to Ivar loudly, but it was no use – there was no sign of him. She wearily shrugged her shoulders at Chloe, who gave Hattie an encouraging smile in return.

'I don't even know if he's in there,' sighed Hattie. 'But I might know a way to find out.

Follow me round to the back. I'll need everyone's help with this.'

Behind the den, Hattie pulled out a handful of the volcanic rocks given to her by the trolls. Then she pointed to a stumpy clay pot resting crookedly on the roof.

'I think that's the chimney,' she explained. 'Billy, Chloe – could you help me to climb up to reach it?'

After two or three attempts, Chloe managed to steady Hattie enough for her to clamber on to Billy's shoulders, and then on to the roof.

'Mith, we need your help!' called Hattie, holding the trolls' rocks in her outstretched palms. 'Could you warm these up, please?'

Mith Ickle fluttered up immediately and gently breathed over the rocks. They soon began to glow, then to smoke – and finally the

heated rocks gave off the worst stench Hattie had ever smelt.

'It's even worse than that time you left those egg sandwiches in your lunch box for the whole of half-term!' said Chloe, pinching her nostrils together tightly.

Holding her breath, Hattie quickly reached up and threw the rocks down the chimney. Then she got down off the roof and waited.

They soon heard angry grunts and clattering sounds coming from inside the den. Seconds later Ivar burst through the door, coughing and spluttering. He staggered around the clearing, a skinny headband tied round his spiky-haired head. The phoenix feather was at the centre of the band!

'*You!* Hattie B!' he cried, pointing a long, sharp fingernail in her direction.

Chloe cowered behind Billy.

'You can't defeat me now, interfering Guardian, no matter how many friends you bring! I'm the all-powerful King Ivar and you're standing in my new kingdom, the Kingdom of the Important Imp Ivar! I'm immortal and you can't stop me! Try as you might, Hattie B, I will always be reborn! Everyone will come under my control now — starting with *you* and —' he jabbed a finger

towards Mith Ickle, Billy and Chloe – 'your meddling friends!'

Then Ivar flapped his small wings, lifted into the air and began circling Hattie and her friends, so that his heavy musty-smelling cape almost brushed their frightened faces.

Hattie felt Chloe's hand grasp her arm. 'We'll be OK,' Hattie said, trying her best to believe her own words.

As Ivar whirled round the clearing, she could tell that his flying skills had improved dramatically since her last visit. Round and round the four friends he went, every swoop bringing him within a whisker of them.

'He'll catch us all if we stay together,' exclaimed Hattie, then more loudly she shouted, 'Everyone, run!'

Without hesitating, Mith Ickle and Billy darted off in opposite directions.

Chloe stayed close to Hattie, clutching her arm tightly. As Ivar swooped towards them, both girls shivered. A definite chill had descended on the forest and, as they looked up, they saw snowflakes were beginning to fall.

A Tough Choice

Mith Ickle was the first to escape Ivar's snowstorm. She soared into the sky and perched on a high branch, watching nervously as the evil imp used his stolen powers to change the weather in the clearing at his whim.

'That silly dragon can wait!' yelled Ivar, narrowing his eyes. 'But you, Hattie B, you're my real prize!'

Hattie could feel her heart thumping in her chest. She thought she heard a small gulp escape from Chloe, who was gripping her arm tighter than ever. Snow was whirling all around them now and great flakes of it were landing on their hair and clothes.

'I can't see where I'm going!' called Chloe.

However, Hattie could barely hear her over the howling wind that was driving the snow into their eyes. She could just about see Billy escape, as he darted across the clearing and into the trees, where he sheltered from the snowstorm out of Ivar's sight.

As the wind grew stronger and the snow heavier, Ivar circled closer and closer round

Hattie and Chloe. Holding hands, the two girls did their best to escape, but it was no use. The snowstorm was pushing them back towards Ivar's den. He was flying faster than ever and cackling so close to their faces that his rotten breath made them cough and splutter.

'You'll never escape now!' he taunted. 'Two silly girls for the price of one!'

Hattie reached into her pocket. If she could just grab one of the startleberries, she might be able to do something . . .

Snap! Whizz! Bang! The berry exploded the moment Hattie threw it at Ivar. But the effect was useless. The noise was drowned out by the whistling winds of the snowstorm.

'Oh no!' cried Chloe, her face full of panic. 'It didn't work!'

'Don't worry – I'll try again!' called Hattie.

She reached into her pocket and this time took out *all* the startleberries. She lifted them above her head against the wind and, aiming

carefully, threw them as hard as she could in the direction of King Ivar.

This time, the berries collided together in one huge, noisy explosion. The flying imp was startled immediately. He dropped awkwardly to the ground, frantically patting his ears to recover from the boom.

With Ivar out of action, the storm weakened enough for Hattie to take her chance. She quickly reached out and grabbed the phoenix feather from Ivar's headband. She placed it carefully in her pocket, which immediately began to glow a gentle purple.

Ivar jumped up suddenly and shook his whole body, from his head to his toes.

'Give that back!' he yelled through disgusting brown clenched teeth. 'It's mine now. Give it back, silly Guardian. NOW!'

Hattie, however, was already running into the trees to join Billy, who greeted her with a happy high five. She turned to check that Chloe was OK – but she wasn't there! She was still by the den, frozen in fear!

'Run, Chloe! Over here!' shouted Hattie.

Chloe had barely taken two steps when Ivar, his face red with anger, began whirling in the air even more furiously. He was building the snowstorm back up!

Hattie watched helplessly as her best friend stumbled on the freshly fallen snow.

Ivar grabbed his chance. He stepped forward with a menacing grin on his face, forcing Chloe further backwards. She had nowhere to go except through Ivar's front door! As the toadstools hissed scarily, Ivar cackled in victory.

'Chloe! Chloe! No!' called Hattie, her voice breaking with terror.

She looked around her for help, but the storm was now so powerful that she could barely see a thing. Ivar had replaced the snow with huge hailstones, which fell continuously from the darkening sky.

Hattie tried to get closer to Ivar's den, but the wind and hail pushed her away until she was actually blown back towards the trees and into an alarmed Billy. An equally worried-looking Mith Ickle flew down to join them.

'I'll never get to her or the other trapped creatures,' said Hattie, fighting back tears.

She looked down at her glowing pocket that held the feather and suddenly Hattie knew exactly what she had to do.

'That's it! I need to heal Magenta so I can give her back the power of rebirth and take it away from Ivar. Come on, Mith, Billy!' cried Hattie, now running. 'We've got to get back to the cave as fast as we can!'

Then she stopped dead in her tracks, her face wrinkled with worry. 'No. I can't leave Chloe here. She must be terrified!'

'I don't think you've got any other choice,' said Mith Ickle gently, curling herself round the Guardian's shoulders.

Chloe's words from earlier rang in Hattie's ears: *I'm trusting you to make a good choice*. Chloe had never had to put so much trust in Hattie before. Was Hattie really making a good choice? She couldn't be sure, but it was the only one she had.

Holding on to a tree trunk to fight the wind, Hattie turned to Ivar and shouted as loudly as she could over the howling storm: 'You'll never win, Ivar! We'll be back – don't you worry. I'll never give up, not until Chloe and all of Bellua are safe!'

Then, hoping Chloe could hear her, she called out as positively as she could: 'Be brave,

Chloe. You have to trust me. I'll come and rescue you as soon as I can – I promise!'

With that, Hattie set off through the Secret Forest with Mith Ickle and Billy – and, for the second time that day, she really hoped she could keep her promise.

The Call for a Cure

As the trio left the Secret Forest, they found the wise sphinxes waiting for them, as if they knew that Hattie would need a swift ride back to the Guardian's cave.

Hattie was cheered by the encouraging calls she heard from every creature they passed, though the image of Chloe's terrified face kept popping into her head.

Back inside the cave, she found Magenta crouched on the stone table, staring down with her head low on her chest. Her bright feathers seemed to have lost even more of their glow since Hattie had left her that morning.

'Hey, Magenta, look what I've got!' called Hattie, pulling the rescued feather from her pocket.

Magenta looked up immediately, her eyes wide. A fiery ripple ran through her plumage.

'Oh, Hattie, you did it! Thank you. Thank you so much!' cried Magenta, ruffling her feathers with excitement.

'All I need to do now is to put your rebirth feather back in place,' said Hattie, reaching for

the red book. 'So . . . how do I do that?'

She scanned the page on phoenixes carefully, waiting patiently for new instructions to appear. But she soon realized no more words were forming on the thick cream paper. Pushing the book to one side, she turned to Magenta.

'I guess I'll have to work it out for myself. Can I have another look at where the missing feather goes?'

Being as gentle as she could, Hattie carefully parted the feathers at the end of Magenta's tail until she spotted the tiny gap in the middle.

'Hmm, I wonder how we can reattach this,' she murmured, bringing the rescued feather closer to the space to check it fitted.

Pop! The feather suddenly jumped into position like a piece of metal on to a magnet, releasing a small purple-tinged puff of ashy smoke as it locked into place.

'Oh no, the ash! Quick, I need something to collect it!' cried Hattie.

'Don't worry. It's not that ash you need,' said Magenta. 'Take a spoonful from *this*!'

Hattie watched in amazement as the magical bird squeezed her eyes shut and burst into a dazzling swirl of flames, right in front of her!

Mith Ickle and Billy gasped, while Hattie stood still, her mouth fixed in a shocked O, as a pile of gently glowing ashes formed on the table. The little phoenix had disappeared completely!

'Collect them now, Hattie, before she's reborn!' urged Mith Ickle, giving her friend a light nudge.

'You can put them in here,' added Billy, holding out a small empty glass jar.

Hattie quickly scooped a spoonful of ash into the jar. She'd just pushed in its tightly fitting cork stopper when the remaining ashes on the table began to pulse bright yellow, then warm orange and finally deep red.

All of a sudden, Magenta burst out of the ashes and the three friends gave a gasp of amazement, even louder than before. Her feathers were brighter than ever now, the yellow and orange flecked with a healthy red as shiny as a ruby. In fact, Magenta's entire body seemed to glow and shimmer, lighting up the whole cave!

Delighted to see the phoenix looking so happy, Hattie turned back to the book.

'Now for Ivar,' she said. 'Unicorn hair and pegasus water. That's what I need now.'

Hattie pulled the beautiful mermaid shell from her pocket and pressed it to her lips. The shiny shell cast a magical golden glow as she softly called, 'Themis! Archie!' She repeated both names to be sure. 'Are you there?'

She was answered by the creak of the cave door opening. In hurried Themis, with the young pegasus trotting behind him.

'You need our help, Guardian?' asked Themis, his deep, rich voice echoing round the cave.

'I just need one of your hairs,' said Hattie. 'And from you, Archie, a little of your spring water, please.'

'Of course, Guardian,' said Themis, and the
unicorn leader lowered his neck so that Hattie
could easily reach the lilac hairs of his silky
mane.

Hattie leant forward and chose the longest and thickest hair she could see. She hoped it wouldn't hurt to take it, but Themis didn't seem to notice as she grasped the strand and pulled. A tiny spark flashed as she plucked it.

Dropping the hair into the phoenix ashes, Hattie turned to Archie.

'I've been practising hard since you healed me,' said Archie. 'Watch!'

'Hold on a minute!' called Hattie, moving to the far end of the cave. She remembered when she'd cured Archie on his last visit to the cave. 'I don't really want a shower this time!'

Archie stamped so hard on the cave floor that there was a light tinkle from the potion bottles on the shelves as they gently knocked into each other. Then a plume of water rose steadily into the air, falling in a shimmering fountain to form a gleaming puddle.

Hattie scooped up a beaker of water as quickly as she could and added it carefully to the ashes and unicorn hair. Then she put the cork stopper back in and swished the magical ingredients around gently.

The contents of the jar immediately took on a glistening pearly glow that rippled with the palest of pinks, blues and greens. Its swirling beauty almost took Hattie's breath away.

'Right, all we have to do now is get this to Ivar,' she said. 'Then I can rescue Chloe and all the other creatures he's managed to trap. Who's coming with me?'

Nobody wanted to be left behind this time. As Hattie hurried through the cave door, Mith Ickle, Billy, Magenta, Themis and Archie quickly filed out behind her.

'To the Secret Forest!' she commanded, like an army captain leading her troops. 'And the defeat of Ivar!'

Gone in a Whisper

The group had only just passed Dragon's Valley when Mith Ickle, flying a little ahead, started snorting with irritation.

'Oh, Hattie! Read the note tied to this bush. And when we're in such a hurry too!'

Hattie stopped and read aloud: '*Beware! Silvery Stream flooded. Go through the Fairy Forest instead, Hattie!*'

Though she was keen to get back to Ivar's den as soon as possible, Hattie tried to live up to her name and stay bright.

'Oh well, it's nice that someone thought to warn me,' she said cheerfully. 'Come on, everyone! We need to take a detour if we want to avoid getting held up by the flood.'

Then she left the path beside the stream and strode towards the Fairy Forest, her friends following.

The fairies were all delighted to see Hattie. This time none pulled at her hair or played silly chasing games round her. Mith Ickle blew out a few puffs of smoke as a warning, but the fairies didn't seem keen on bothering her either.

'We're so glad you're here to help, Hattie,' they called instead. Several sprinkled fairy dust, which twinkled in Hattie's long dark hair and added a light shimmer to the single white

streak that marked her out as a Guardian. 'We really hope you can free our trapped friends.'

'Me too!' called Hattie, weaving round trees covered in delicate yellow and green leaves as she made her way through the forest.

She held on tight to her jar of precious ingredients, thinking of just one thing – getting to her best friend as quickly as possible.

Hanging from a low branch on one particularly tall tree was a second sign. It was swinging lightly and written in the same neat blue writing as the first one she'd seen:

Rumbling Volcano rumbling!
Keep behind it, Hattie!

'The volcano rarely erupts,' said Themis, looking concerned. 'But when all is not well in Bellua the land shows its sickness. The note is right – any lava is certain to collect at the front of the mountain. If we stay behind it, we should be safe.'

'Don't worry, Hattie. We'll still get to the Secret Forest, just from the other side,' added Billy, on whose shoulders Magenta had hitched a ride again.

'OK, I trust you both,' said Hattie. 'Come on – let's go!'

After a few minutes, the forest began to get denser and the branches were harder and harder to part.

Hattie was cheered slightly by the notes nailed to every third or fourth tree trunk. Some showed only a simple arrow, while others said *This way!* or *Keep going!* However, the second time Hattie came across what she thought was the same note, she began to

wonder if the directions were really helping her after all . . .

Suddenly, Hattie stopped so abruptly that Themis bumped right into her, causing Billy to trip into Themis, and Archie to tumble into Billy, which sent Magenta flying off her shoulder perch.

'Oops! Sorry,' whispered Hattie, 'but I think I can see where all these notes have been leading – right into that pen over there!'

Hattie pointed towards a small clearing in the dense forest. In the middle of it was a round pen, the sort that Hattie had seen lambs held in at a local petting farm. The fence was made from crooked branches, poking out of a thick scattering of leaves and twigs, and in the middle of the pen was a tall pile of more leaves. As she tiptoed closer, something else caught Hattie's eye. The pile of leaves seemed to be quivering, and poking out of it were a few wisps of hair. Bright blue hair.

'Shhhhhh!' said Hattie to her friends, cupping her ear as she leant forward. 'I'm sure there's someone in those leaves. I can hear talking!'

'Oh, King Ivar's going to be so proud of my brilliant plan! Hattie B and all her friends, trapped in my hidden pen!'

Hattie instantly recognized the giggling voice that was coming from the leaves.

'Immie!' whispered Hattie in alarm. 'There really is nothing that silly imp won't do to help Ivar!'

'So she led us here on purpose,' said Themis gravely.

'And hid in the leaves while she waited for us to arrive, the cheeky imp!' added Billy.

'What do you think she planned to do with us, Hattie?' asked Mith Ickle.

Hattie shook her head. 'I'm not exactly sure but I don't think we'll hang around to find out!' she said. 'Everyone, keep really quiet. We don't want Immie to know we're here yet.'

Quietly, Hattie pulled out the spool of shimmer-spider thread and handed it to Billy.

'I'll take the end and we'll run round and round the pen until it's completely covered. Then it'll be Immie who's trapped instead of us. She won't be able to distract us again,' she said, setting to work.

With Mith Ickle and Magenta flying silently back and forth, lifting the thread over and under itself, the pen was soon completely criss-crossed with a dense and very sticky web. A perfect trap for Immie!

'Fine work, Hattie,' whispered Themis, as she and Billy stepped back and admired their handiwork.

'Let's go before Immie spots us,' said Hattie, but it was too late.

Immie burst out of the leaves and began darting about around the pen, getting more entangled in the spider's thread as she went.

She tried hard to escape the pen, but the sticky thread caught on her clothes and hair, sending her into a wild fury.

'Let me out of here!' she yelled. 'I'm not supposed to be stuck in here, Hattie B. YOU are! Ivar ordered me to keep you here for a very long time – a hostage of the Kingdom of the Important Imp Ivar!'

'Well, you're definitely stuck now, Immie!' called Hattie, laughing. With that, she turned away from Immie and rushed off through the forest, with her friends close behind.

Hattie expected dazzling light to greet them once they left the trees of the dense forest behind, so she was surprised to find that Bellua's usually bright sky had turned dusky blue. She'd never been in Bellua at night-time! It was the first time she'd seen the large round moon in Bellua's sky. It looked like the one she was used to seeing at home, except it was the palest pink, as though it was made from soft marshmallow.

The small group cast shadows on the path as they made their way round the Rumbling Volcano and towards the Secret Forest.

It was getting darker by the second and Hattie felt a flicker of fear. She'd never stayed in Bellua this late before. She comforted herself with the thought that she had nothing to fear with most of the creatures on her side.

However, for Chloe, that was a different matter. Hattie thought of her best friend held by Ivar in the darkening forest, and quickened her pace. She had to get there as soon as she could. Her best friend, Chloe, and all the creatures of Bellua were relying on her.

Hattie's Plea

It was even darker in the Secret Forest. Hattie dropped back and let Billy lead the way to Ivar's den, grateful for Mith Ickle breathing out occasional bursts of fire to light the way. In the gloom, the Secret Forest felt even more menacing than before. The air was still and silent, and every twig that cracked under Hattie's feet made her jump.

They came to the clearing sooner than she had expected. Hattie looked all around but there was no sign of Ivar – or Chloe. The captive creatures began to murmur with excitement when they spotted Hattie.

'Let's free as many as we can straight away,' said Hattie, turning to her friends.

The group scattered quickly, anxious to break the ropes and posts that were keeping the prisoners trapped. Mith Ickle used her fire to burn through one piece of rope, which freed not one but two young unicorns. Meanwhile Billy tore several bonds apart with his horns, releasing a whole host of pixies, elves and sprites. With Themis using his great strength to knock over the wooden posts, the clearing was soon full of grateful creatures. But there was still no sign of Chloe.

Hattie felt terrible. She shouldn't have let Chloe stay in Bellua after all. What if Ivar had harmed her in some way? Or what if Hattie never found her again?

She tried to ignore the hiss of the toadstools as she approached Ivar's front door. Hattie had almost reached it when she heard a shout from behind her, loud enough to make her stumble forward.

'Hattie!' called Billy. 'Watch out! It's Ivar!'

She had barely steadied herself before Ivar loomed in front of her, jumping from his mossy camouflage on the den's wall – a trick he'd taken from the mermaids.

She gasped and clutched the precious potion jar more tightly. She noticed that Ivar was still wearing the band round his head, though he'd replaced the missing feather with a thin green leaf. Hattie almost laughed at how ridiculous he looked.

'Give me back my feather!' snarled Ivar.

Hattie wrinkled her nose as his rotten breath hit her face.

'It's not your feather – it's Magenta's,' she replied. 'You'll never get it back now, so don't even try!'

The Imp King began to stamp his long feet.

'But *I'm* the supreme leader of Bellua now and I *must* have that feather!' he spat.

Hattie took a step or two backwards as Ivar waved his skinny arms at the magical beings that now filled the clearing.

'All the creatures of Bellua must return to me and pledge their loyalty. NOW! Even you, Hattie B, must bow to my authority. All of you are part of my new kingdom!'

Then, without warning, Ivar rose into the air and began circling Hattie, still proclaiming loudly that he was Ivar, King of the Imps and of all the creatures of the magical Kingdom of Bellua.

'Well, if you will not obey me, you must be

my captive, Hattie B!' he declared, swirling closer and closer to her.

However, Ivar hadn't considered the rescued creatures gathered in the clearing, and the loyalty they all felt towards their Guardian.

Fairies and sprites flew between him and Hattie, grabbing his hair, his cloak and even his long pointy nose. Though Ivar flapped his tiny wings urgently, he could neither get away nor reach out his bony arms far enough to grab them.

When a couple of pegasi took to the air and began circling closely round him too, Ivar found he could barely move at all. He tried sending out flashes of light, another trick he'd stolen from the mermaids. However, the flashes were quickly blocked by puffs of smoke and jets of fire from Mith Ickle and several other dragons, which soon sent him off course.

At last, Ivar seemed to tire and with a frustrated roar he landed on the ground, where several elves began jumping on his toes. Then two unicorns circled him, their heads dipped so that their magical pointed horns were poking into Ivar's furious face.

Finally Billy poked him so hard on the bottom with his horns that Ivar's yelp echoed through the forest. Hattie stifled a laugh as Ivar's face turned redder than ever.

'I'm taking you prisoner, Hattie B. I'm the great and almighty King Ivar, and nobody can stand in my way!' he yelled, staring directly into Hattie's eyes.

'Really, Ivar?' shouted Hattie, trying to hide the small tremble of fear in her voice. 'Is that what you want? To make everyone in this beautiful land miserable? Wouldn't you like to stop being mean, just for once?'

Hattie knew it was a desperate attempt to win Ivar over, but she couldn't help noticing that his twisted face softened slightly.

However, the change didn't last long before Ivar began to cackle menacingly again.

Now was the moment! thought Hattie.

She popped the stopper from the potion jar and, quick as a flash, she threw its contents over the unsuspecting imp.

The shimmering liquid swirled round and round the Imp King as he shrieked and stumbled backwards. He tried to run away but found that he couldn't move. Ivar was stuck fast to the ground, with the magic potion whirling round his feet.

Hattie and her friends watched as the liquid began to rise, turning from red to blue, then green to yellow.

Soon Ivar was barely visible inside the colourful swirl. Everyone watched in silence as the liquid slowly turned to a grey mist that spiralled upward, past Ivar's legs, up his body and then above his head. It carried on rising, floating across the den and over the treetops until it disappeared completely.

Ivar lay slumped on the ground by Hattie's feet, completely covered by his vast cloak.

'Ivar?' whispered Hattie, bending down. 'Ivar, are you all right?'

All Change!

All the creatures stood in a silent circle round Hattie as they waited to see what would happen next. For a minute or two, there was no movement, then Hattie spotted a slight ripple in the cloak's material as Ivar slowly poked his head out.

Not wishing to take any chances, Hattie took a couple of steps back and brought her hands up to her eyes, peering through her fingers to see what Ivar might do next.

At first glance, she thought Ivar looked much the same, though there was no scowl on his face and Hattie could see a rosy blush starting to spread across his cheeks.

'Ivar?' she asked again cautiously.

She was answered by a huge yawn, as though the imp was waking up from the longest sleep ever. He stretched his arms above his head and Hattie noticed that his fingers were chubbier and his nails clean and short.

Staring at his face, she watched in amazement as his pointed nose shrank, turning into a cute snub. Even his beard transformed from ragged wisps into softer curls. The spiky crown that had been perched on top of his head also flew off. In its place, a cuter crown appeared in a puff of smoke with a loud *ping*. He was beginning to look more like a garden gnome than an evil bully!

A ripple of applause spread round the circle of creatures as Ivar slowly stood up. As he did so, his huge cloak transformed before their eyes, lifting off the ground until it reached just below his waist. Its normally dull greeny-brown colour began to fade and was replaced by a cheerful red to match the trim on the smart green suit he now wore beneath it.

As the applause grew louder, a broad smile

spread across Ivar's face and Hattie was pleased to see that even the points on his teeth had disappeared – and they no longer looked like they hadn't been brushed for several years!

'Three cheers for Hattie!' boomed the voice of Themis across the clearing. 'Hip, hip –'

The *hooray* that followed was so loud it echoed throughout the forest, so that by the third cheer the gathered crowd had grown in size considerably.

The noise had only just died down when a softly cautious voice came from behind the half-open door of Ivar's den: 'Is it safe to come out yet?'

'Chloe!' cried Hattie, running to her friend.

The moss had disappeared from the walls, which were now a sunny yellow, and the clean windows were framed by neat red-checked curtains. There were no hissing toadstools as

Hattie approached, only pretty pots of brightly coloured flowers that gave off the sweetest of scents. Even the night sky had brightened. Thousands of stars lit the forest, so it wasn't nearly as scary any more.

'Oh, Hattie, I'm so pleased to see you!' cried Chloe, emerging from the den and throwing her arms round her best friend. 'I was so scared! I didn't know what to do or when I'd see you again and –'

Hattie squeezed Chloe tightly as the sound of Ivar clearing his throat interrupted them.

He slowly got to his feet and looked around, taking in the hundreds of creatures that were staring right back at him.

'Got anything to say for yourself then, Ivar?' called a large hairy troll from the centre of the crowd. A chorus of agreement spread through the gathered creatures.

'Well, I, er, um . . .' began Ivar, looking down at the ground sheepishly.

'Perhaps saying sorry to everyone you've harmed would be a good start?' suggested Hattie gently.

A murmur from the crowd grew louder and louder as every creature joined the call for an apology.

'I, er . . . I'm not entirely sure what I can say, Guardian,' said Ivar, his eyes still fixed to the ground.

'How about "I'm sorry"?' shouted a second troll.

Ivar coughed loudly. 'I am sorry, truly sorry,' he said, looking at the crowd again. 'I never wanted to cause so much suffering, really. I didn't even enjoy being mean all the time, I promise – and as for the cackling, well, my throat's never been so sore! I'm not too sure about the flying either, if I'm honest. That cloak was so heavy!'

Ivar swished his new lighter cloak and ran his fingers through his newly tidy beard before continuing. 'Something made me think I wanted all those magical powers, but now I can see they were never mine to have. The powers belong to all of you and it took a very special Guardian to make me see it.'

He gave a little leap of joy and clasped Hattie's hands in gratitude.

'Hattie B, you are a great Guardian. You're determined and caring – and possibly the greatest Guardian we've ever had! All of us in Bellua are lucky to have you – especially me.'

Hattie wanted to say something in return but she could feel a small lump forming in her throat. She was saved by another creature, who came running into the clearing and screeching at top volume.

'King Ivar! King Ivar? That miserable Guardian's on to you again. I tried to stop her, really I did, but . . . please just give me another task, Your Majesty. I'll do anything. *Anything*. King Ivar? Your Royal Highness . . . *Where ARE you?*'

Immie let out a loud sigh and sat on a tree stump, turning her head from side to side. Hattie could see clumps of the shimmer spiders' thread in her blue hair and all over her clothes.

'I'm right here, you silly thing,' said Ivar.

Immie's mouth fell open and stayed there.

'Hattie's saved me, and you too, little Immie,' he said. 'I've only got one thing left I'm going to ask you to do: think of a way to pay back all these creatures for the trouble and suffering we've caused them.'

For a moment Immie looked at Ivar as though he'd gone mad, but when she turned round Hattie thought she saw a small smile cross Immie's lips.

Ivar urged the blue-haired imp to go home, so Immie left the circle and weaved through the trees, muttering as she went. 'A party maybe? Yes, a party for everyone, with sparkle squash and twinkly treats and a game of pass-the-pumpkin . . .'

'Thanks, Ivar, though I only did what any Guardian would do,' said Hattie. 'Anyway, I really couldn't have done this without the help of *all* the amazing creatures in Bellua – the unicorns and the pegasi, the mermaids, fairies, elves and sprites, the spiders and sphinxes, the dragons and, *oh*, anyone else I've forgotten! And Mith and Billy, of course!' Hattie paused as the creatures of Bellua burst into applause and cheers. Her voice could barely be heard as she added, 'But now I think it's time I said goodbye – I think my friend Chloe's had quite enough excitement for one day!'

Ivar smiled at Chloe apologetically and, following a nudge from Hattie, Chloe gave him a brief smile back.

Hattie didn't know how to say goodbye to an imp who, until very recently, had been her arch-enemy. But Ivar soon took care of her doubts. Throwing his arms round her, he gave Hattie such a large hug it nearly knocked her off her feet. Billy and Mith Ickle stepped forward protectively, just in case – they weren't going to let any harm come to their Hattie B!

'See you then, Ivar,' said Hattie, once he'd let her go. With a laugh, she added, 'And I might even miss you this time!'

A Final Farewell?

'What a day!' said Hattie, as she reached the edge of the Secret Forest, a whole line of creatures following behind.

She accepted Themis's offer of a ride back to the cave. Beside her, Chloe held on tightly to Arlon, Archie's dad, and they were joined by Lunar, the purple and silver unicorn who Hattie had healed on a previous visit.

'Bet you never thought you'd ride on a real pegasus!' called Hattie, but Chloe was too speechless to answer.

The night air in Bellua was lighter than before and a twinkling trail of stars seemed to weave across the sky, as though someone was waving thousands of tiny sparklers through it.

News of Hattie's victory spread throughout Bellua with lightning speed. Every creature that she passed shouted out its thanks and congratulations. Many even joined the end of the procession, eager to take part in the celebrations!

A group of song sprites accompanied her all the way along the Silvery Stream, singing her

praises in a medley of pretty tunes. Hattie eventually lost count of how many fairies sprinkled her with fairy dust, though she was delighted to see that one of them was Titch, the fairy whose wing she'd healed on her third visit to Bellua.

Once they passed through Unicorn Meadows and reached the entrance to the Guardian's cave, Themis and Arlon lowered their necks so that Hattie and Chloe could slide off and join Mith Ickle, Billy, Archie and Magenta.

'It's just like a carnival!' said Chloe, staring in awe at the huge crowd of colourful creatures that had followed them back.

'I know,' agreed Hattie, 'and I'll be even

sadder to leave Bellua behind this time. But we can't stay here forever. It's time we said our goodbyes.'

Mith Ickle curled sadly round Hattie's shoulders as she turned to address the crowd.

'Creatures of Bellua, I'm so glad I could help you all,' she began, as a large two-headed dragon called out, 'Hear, hear!'

'And I'm really pleased that I can say goodbye,' Hattie continued, 'knowing that you're all safe from any more of Ivar's evil plans. I hope that when I next see you all, whenever that might be, it will be in happier times for Bellua!'

Then she called out, 'Bye for now!'

As all the creatures waved and cheered, Hattie led the way into the cave, with Chloe, Mith Ickle, Billy and Magenta following behind.

The first thing Hattie did was take the cork-stoppered jar from her pocket. She'd thrown most of the potion over Ivar but, holding it up, she could see a few drops left in the bottom.

'Well, you never know . . .' she said, and carefully placed it in a small gap on the cave shelves. Then she turned round and cried out, 'Magenta?'

The phoenix was crouching on the stone table and Hattie could see a small cloud of ash forming all round her.

'You're not going to be reborn again, are you?' asked Hattie uncertainly.

Magenta shook her head and flew over to Hattie.

'Not today!' she said, laughing, as the ash

drifted away to reveal a tiny twinkling phoenix

charm, which she dropped into Hattie's palm. 'Thank you so much for curing me, Hattie.'

'And thank you for my beautiful charm, Magenta,' said Hattie, attaching it to her bracelet, where it joined the six charms already hanging there.

Chloe laughed. 'Ah! So that's where they all came from!'

Hattie grinned and said, 'At least now I don't have to explain every time I get a new one!'

With that, Hattie knew it really was time to go. As she reached for the vet's bag, she felt Mith Ickle curl herself round her shoulders, whispering a melodic goodbye.

'Bye, Mith. Now I've taken care of Ivar, I really don't know when I'll be back.' Hattie felt her eyes moisten a little. 'But I hope it won't be too long,' she added, stroking Mith Ickle's head gently.

Hattie turned to the others. 'Bye, Magenta,' she said. 'And thanks for your help with the ashes. Billy, see you soon – I hope!'

Billy gave Hattie a friendly high five, and Chloe too, and then his face grew more serious. 'See you then, Hattie. With Ivar defeated, I hope there won't be any more trouble . . .'

Hattie glanced at the seven charms now swinging on her bracelet. 'You know I'll be back the moment any of these glow. You can count on it!' she said, meaning every word.

She looked at her vet's bag. If she'd been worried about Chloe following her to Bellua, she was even more worried about her not being able to leave again.

'So you just peered into the bag and that was it?' asked Hattie.

Chloe smiled and nodded.

'I looked inside and saw your feet disappearing – and then I started falling into it as well!'

'OK,' said Hattie. 'Let's try to go back together. We'll hold hands and, when I count to three, we'll lean into the bag as far as we can. *One . . . two . . . three!'*

With Mith Ickle, Billy and Magenta's final goodbyes ringing in their ears, both girls leant over the open bag.

And in less than a second the two friends felt themselves tumbling down, down and down . . .

Telling Tales

Hattie and Chloe couldn't help rolling into each other as they both bounced back on to Hattie's bed at once. Chloe quickly pulled herself upright, then cupped her face in both hands.

'Oh no, Hattie – your mum!' she exclaimed. 'Won't she be wondering where on earth we've been? We'll have missed tea and everything.'

Hattie smiled. 'Check the clock,' she replied, pointing to her clock's digital display.

Chloe stared at it in amazement.

'I can be in Bellua *all* day and when I get back it's like I never left my room,' Hattie explained. 'Quite useful really. My mum and dad and Peter don't know anything about it.'

'Wow, that's quite a secret to keep from your big brother,' said Chloe. 'What if Peter ever catches you leaving – you know, like I did?'

'He'd have to get into my room first!' laughed Hattie. Then in a more serious voice she said, 'You mustn't ever tell him though, Chloe. Or anyone. Promise?'

Chloe nodded.

'It's just there's this oath, a secret one,' Hattie continued. 'I suppose I've sort of broken it now, but, well, it was only by accident and I know I can trust you, Chloe. I mean we're best friends forever, aren't we?'

Chloe squeezed her hand and Hattie knew that if there was one person in the world she could always trust, it was Chloe.

'So, the charms glow and that's when you know it's time to go back to Bellua?'

Hattie nodded. She and Chloe were lying side by side on the bed, their heads propped up on a pile of soft animal-shaped cushions. Hattie had promised to tell Chloe anything she wanted to know – and Chloe wanted to know *everything*!

'Is that where you went that time we did the show in the village hall then? And before Sports Club that day?'

Hattie nodded again.

'Well, that explains it then!' Chloe laughed. 'I mean, at the time I just thought you were being really *weird*!'

'Thanks!' said Hattie, giving Chloe a playful tap on the shoulder.

'Do you think you'll get in any trouble for letting me come with you?' asked Chloe, but before Hattie could answer there was a light

knock on her bedroom door and a smiling face
peered round it.

'Uncle B!' exclaimed Hattie. 'I didn't know
you were here!'

'Ah well, people turn up in the strangest places,' replied Uncle B, glancing at Chloe and winking. 'And I turned up here with a rumbling tummy just when your mum was putting a delicious pie in the oven. Perfect timing!'

Uncle B paused and ran his fingers through his dark hair, just missing the white streak that ran down one side of it.

'So, Hattie,' he continued, 'I hear congratulations are in order, eh? Seems you've brought a lot of happiness to Bellua today and made your old uncle very proud indeed.'

Hattie felt herself blush slightly. 'Well, I only –' she began.

But Uncle B jumped in. 'You only did exactly what I knew you would – exactly what I would have once done. I always knew you were the perfect choice to take over from me. You really have proved yourself to be a most excellent Guardian. I hear the creatures are most grateful. Well done, you!'

Hattie could see Chloe looking at her and Uncle B, but it was Uncle B who spoke.

'Now, Chloe, this must all seem very strange to you, I'm sure. You must have had quite an adventure today, but no harm done, eh?'

'I didn't mean to . . .' began Hattie.

Uncle B waved her words away with his hand. 'As I said, no harm done,' he insisted.

'Sometimes these things happen for the best of reasons. You're in no trouble, dear Hattie.'

Hattie felt relieved, but there was still something bothering her.

'Uncle B,' she said, 'how do you always know what's going on in Bellua?'

Uncle B tapped his nose mysteriously. 'Aha,' he replied. 'Once you've been to Bellua, it *always* stays with you somehow or other. You'll know such things too one day, my dear.

'Speaking of which,' he continued, 'I've heard that something's been causing trouble in the mountains, but that could just be a rumour . . .'

Before Hattie could ask him anything more,

he pushed the bedroom door open wide and said, 'All you need to know for now, Hattie, is that the delicious smell of your mum's shepherd's pie is drifting up the stairs. If we don't go downstairs and eat it soon, we'll all be in trouble!'

Once the shepherd's pie had been eaten and Uncle B had said a cheery goodbye, Chloe's dad arrived to take her home.

'Bye, Hattie,' said Chloe, giving her friend a tight hug. Then she whispered in her ear, 'And thanks for letting me share the best adventure *ever*!'

Hattie smiled. It had certainly been an adventure – and sharing it with Chloe had made it the best one she'd had in Bellua so far.

As she hugged her best friend, the charms on Hattie's bracelet jangled against each other. Would they ever glow again and call her back to Bellua?

Waving Chloe goodbye, Hattie couldn't help hoping they would . . .

Hattie's Trail

Which path must Hattie follow to reach the Rumbling Volcano?

A

B

C

Hattie B
Magical Vet

Find out more about

Hattie B

and the creatures

from the

Kingdom of

Bellua

by visiting

www.worldofhattieb.com

Listen

Do you love listening to stories?

Want to know what happens behind the scenes in a recording studio?

Hear funny sound effects, exclusive author interviews and the best books read by famous authors and actors on the **Puffin Podcast** at **www.puffinbooks.com**

#ListenWithPuffin

It all started with a Scarecrow

Puffin is over seventy years old.
Sounds ancient, doesn't it? But Puffin has never been
so lively. We're always on the lookout for the next big
idea, which is how it began all those years ago.

Penguin Books was a big idea from the mind of
a man called Allen Lane, who in 1935 invented
the quality paperback and changed the world.
**And from great Penguins, great Puffins grew,
changing the face of children's books forever.**

The first four Puffin Picture Books were hatched in 1940 and the
first Puffin story book featured a man with broomstick arms called
Worzel Gummidge. In 1967 Kaye Webb, Puffin Editor, started the
Puffin Club, promising to **'make children into readers'**.
She kept that promise and over 200,000 children became devoted
Puffineers through their quarterly instalments of *Puffin Post*.

Many years from now, we hope you'll look back and
remember Puffin with a smile. **No matter what your age
or what you're into, there's a Puffin for everyone.**
The possibilities are endless, but one thing is for sure:
whether it's a picture book or a paperback, a sticker book
or a hardback, **if it's got that little Puffin
on it – it's bound to be good.**